HENRY HECKELBECK

and the Great Frog Escape

By **Wanda Coven**

Illustrated by **Priscilla Burris**

LITTLE SIMON

New York   London   Toronto   Sydney   New Delhi

LITTLE SIMON
An imprint of Simon & Schuster Children's Publishing Division
1230 Avenue of the Americas, New York, New York 10020
First Little Simon paperback edition December 2022
Copyright © 2022 by Simon & Schuster, Inc.
Also available in a Little Simon hardcover edition.
All rights reserved, including the right of reproduction in whole or in part in any form. LITTLE SIMON is a registered trademark of Simon & Schuster, Inc., and associated colophon is a trademark of Simon & Schuster, Inc.
For information about special discounts for bulk purchases, please contact Simon & Schuster Special Sales at 1-866-506-1949 or business@simonandschuster.com. The Simon & Schuster Speakers Bureau can bring authors to your live event. For more information or to book an event contact the Simon & Schuster Speakers Bureau at 1-866-248-3049 or visit our website at www.simonspeakers.com.
Designed by Leslie Mechanic
Manufactured in the United States of America 1122 LAK
10 9 8 7 6 5 4 3 2 1
Library of Congress Cataloging-in-Publication Data | Names: Coven, Wanda, author. | Burris, Priscilla, illustrator. | Title: Henry Heckelbeck and the great frog escape / by Wanda Coven ; illustrated by Priscilla Burris. | Description: First Little Simon paperback edition. | New York : Little Simon, 2022. | Series: Henry Heckelbeck ; 11 | Audience: Ages 5-9. | Summary: When Henry accidentally brings a frog home from Brewster Creek he plans to return it the next day, but things quickly turn chaotic when the frog escapes, and now Henry must try everything, even magic, to catch the energetic amphibian. | Identifiers: LCCN 2022026900 (print) | LCCN 2022026901 (ebook) | ISBN 9781665933704 (paperback) | ISBN 9781665933711 (hardcover) | ISBN 9781665933728 (ebook) | Subjects: CYAC: Frogs—Fiction. | Magic—Fiction. | Classification: LCC PZ7.C83393 Hnm 2022(print) | LCC PZ7.C83393 (ebook) | DDC [Fic]—dc23 | LC record available at https://lccn.loc.gov/2022026900
LC ebook record available at https://lccn.loc.gov/2022026901

CONTENTS

Chapter 1
THE FROG KING

Chugga-wump!

Chugga-wump-wump!

Henry *heard* the frog. Now he just had to *find* it. He peeked in between the tall grasses and scanned the lily pads.

Chugga-wump!

Henry slowly looked from side to side. Then he gasped. There, sitting on a large lily pad, was an enormous bullfrog.

Whoa! Henry thought. *This must be the Frog King of Brewster Creek!*

Henry crept from behind the grasses and stepped into the shallow water. He could feel the cold water through his rubber boots.

"I have to catch you, Frog King!" Henry whispered. "My friends won't believe it!"

He took another small step forward and raised his net.  The frog didn't budge from his lily pad throne. It was going to work! Henry was going to catch that frog!

He was about to bring the net down when somebody shouted, "HEY, HENRY!"

PLOP! The Frog King hopped into the water and escaped.

"Merg!" Henry cried.

Dudley splashed up the
creek toward his friend. "Did
you get anything?"

Henry chucked the net onto
the bank. "No. You scared it
away by yelling!"

"Scared WHAT away?" asked Dudley.

Henry folded his arms. "My king-size FROG!"

Dudley covered his mouth with his hand. "Oops! Sorry, dude! I didn't catch any either."

Max splashed up to the boys, held out her bucket, and cheered, "Well, I caught THREE!"

The boys groaned and looked in the bucket. Her frogs were small, but they were frogs.

"Nice going, Max," said Henry. Then his stomach growled.

Both Dudley and Max heard it and laughed.

"Did you swallow a frog?" Max asked.

Henry rubbed his hand in a circle on his stomach. "No, I'm just super hungry," he said. "Want to have lunch?"

The friends agreed. Max walked to the edge of the creek and tipped her bucket on its side.

Plip! Plop! Plip!

Henry watched all of Max's frogs hop into the water and wondered what would have happened if his frog hadn't gotten away.

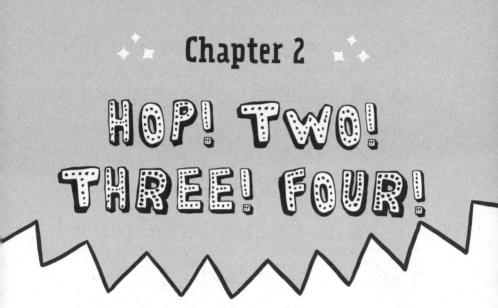

Chapter 2

HOP! TWO! THREE! FOUR!

"Did you catch a frog?" asked Mom, who had lunch ready on a picnic table.

Henry sighed and grabbed a turkey sandwich.

"Almost," he said.

Max popped a grape in her mouth and said, "Frogs can be VERY slippery, you know."

"I hear they scare easily too," said Dudley as he pulled open his chip bag.

Henry gave that joke a fake laugh. "Hardy har."

When the friends finished eating, Max pulled out a deck of cards. The cards had a picture of a frog sitting on a lily pad. Above the frog, it said *I just really like frogs, okay?!*

"So, who wants to play Go Frog?" asked Max. "It's the same as Go Fish, only with frogs!"

Dudley's hand shot up. "I DO!"

Henry slid off the bench and grabbed his net and bucket. "Thanks, but I'm going to try and catch a real frog one more time before we go."

"Better hop to it!" Mom said. "It looks like rain, and I don't want to get stuck out here in a storm."

"Okay," said Henry as he headed for the creek.

"You've TOAD-ally got this!" Dudley shouted.

Henry walked back to the same spot. He pulled back the grasses. *No frogs in here.*

He checked the tops of the lily pads. *No frogs out there, either.*

"Oh well," he said, turning to leave.

Chugga-wump!

Henry whirled back around. Sitting on the bank beside him was the Frog King.

"Well, hello, Your Royal Froggyness!" Henry said.

"*Chugga-wump-wump!*" the Frog King answered.

Henry bent over and gently wrapped his hands around the plump frog. He lifted the frog to his face.

"You're a beauty!" Henry
told him. "Want to meet my
friends?"

Henry was about to lower the frog into his bucket when the car horn blared. *HONK! Honk, honk!*

The sound frightened Henry,
who let go of the frog and
watched it hop away.

"HENRY! We're LEAVING!"
Mom called.

Henry looked at his magnificent frog. The frog looked back at Henry.

"*Chugga-wump!*" it croaked.

"I'm sorry. I have to go," Henry said.

Then he ran to the car, packed his frogging gear in the trunk, and hopped in the back seat. Little did he know, something else had hopped into the car too.

Boing!

Boing!

Boing!

Chapter 3

KER-THUNK!

"Let's go to MY room!" Henry said when they got home.

The friends ran upstairs. Max plunked onto a beanbag chair and sighed. "I miss my frogs," she said, shutting her eyes.

"I can almost hear them saying they miss me too." Max pretended to listen for frogs.

"Chugga-wump!" croaked a *real* frog.

"Wow, you have a great imagination, Max!" Dudley said. "Because I just heard a frog croak too."

BOING!

Suddenly the Frog King leaped onto Henry's bed.

"You DID hear a frog," said Henry. "But it's not one of Max's frogs. It's MY frog."

Dudley and Max ran over.

"Wowee! Whoa! How'd that humongous frog get on your BED?" cried Dudley.

Max wedged herself between the boys so she could see.

"It's the size of all three of my frogs in ONE!" she said.

Henry smiled proudly. "Meet the Frog King of Brewster Creek!"

Dudley and Max looked at
each other with wide eyes.

"Dude, how'd you even
get this frog IN here?" asked
Dudley.

Henry puffed his chest out—
just a little. "A good spy NEVER
reveals their secrets."

Max frowned. "So, in other
words, you don't know."

Henry unpuffed
his chest. "Yup,
I have absolutely
no idea," he
admitted. "It must
have followed
me home."

"Well, that is one smart frog!" said Dudley with a bow. "May I be the first to welcome you to Henry's bedroom, Your Royal Hoppingness?"

Henry laughed. "He does look kingly, right?!"

Max took a closer look. "He does seem very old and wise."

"Chugga-wump!" croaked the frog, and the kids burst into laughter. It was almost as if the frog understood what Max had said.

"How will you get the Frog King BACK to the creek?" asked Dudley.

Henry shrugged. "Hmm, it's raining now, so . . . we can bring him back tomorrow, I guess," he suggested.

"What about tonight?" asked Max.

Henry placed the Frog King in his bucket on top of his desk. "He'll be safe in here tonight," he said. "Besides, how hard can it be to babysit a frog?"

Suddenly a new sound came from Henry's desk. *Ker-thunk!* The bucket had fallen over.

"Uh, what just happened?" asked Henry.

"Um," said Max, "I think the Frog King just escaped."

Chapter 4
BETTER GET HOPPIN'

"Where did he go?" Henry asked.

Dudley and Max looked around the room, but the Frog King was nowhere to be found.

"That is one sneaky frog!" said Dudley. "First he escaped Brewster Creek, then he hitched a ride to your house, and now he's given us the slip!"

"Guys, it's time to conduct a Missing Frog Investigation," said Max. "Spread out! Henry, check under the furniture. Dudley, search the closet. I'll take the bookshelves."

The three spies began to investigate. Henry dropped to his knees and looked under the bed. Dudley looked in all four corners of the closet.

"No amphibians in here!" Dudley called out.

Max pulled books from the bookshelves. *Thump! Slap! Thwack!* She stacked them in a pile. "No frogs in between the books!" she called out.

Henry pulled his head out from under his desk. "No frogs under the furniture either," he said. "Where else could it be?"

"*Chugga-wump-wump!*" croaked the frog.

Dudley pointed
toward Henry's
bedroom door.
"Looks like
your royal
frog is about
to check out of
the Henry Hotel!"

The Frog King was sitting
by the door. It stared back at
the kids with wide eyes and a
froggy smile.

"WAIT!" Henry cried.

But it was too late. The Frog King had already hopped into the hall and started to go downstairs.

"We have a runner!" Max cried as all three friends raced for the door. "Or should I say, a *hopper*?!"

Chapter 5

HIP HOP!

As Henry raced after the frog, the thoughts in his head raced even faster.

What if the frog pees on the carpet?! What if my parents SEE the frog in the HOUSE?!

What if someone accidentally STEPS on the frog?!

Henry blazed down the stairs while Dudley and Max stood guard at the top of the stairs in case the Frog King tried to sneak back.

"Henry? Is that you?" called Mom from the kitchen.

Henry and the frog *froze* on the bottom stair.

"Yup! It's just me and NOBODY ELSE!" said Henry. His voice sounded weirdly high-pitched.

"Your teacher, Ms. Mizzle, stopped by!" said Mom. "Tell your friends to come down for snacks and a visit."

Normally Henry would love a surprise visit from his teacher, but NOT in the middle of a full-on frog chase.

Henry thought fast. "Um, I need to change into a fancy shirt!" he said as he reached down and wrapped his hands around the frog's plump body.

"Gotcha!" he whispered as he heard his mom's shoes click toward the hallway. Henry hid the frog behind his back.

"You look *fine*," said Mom, waving Henry into the kitchen. "Come say hello."

Henry held the squirming frog tightly as he walked over and poked his head around the corner.

"Hi, Ms. Mizzle! Nice to see you!" he said. "Let me go get Dudley and Max, okay?"

Then Henry backed away before Ms. Mizzle or his mom could say anything.

But as soon as he was out of their view, the frog sprang

from his hands like a wet bar of soap.

Hip hop! Hippity hop!

Henry watched as the Frog King hopped right into the kitchen!

Chapter 6
COME BACK HERE!

Oh NO! I'm in froggy trouble now! Henry thought.

But maybe there was one way to help: his magic book!

Henry closed his eyes and made a wish.

When Henry opened his eyes, there was a shimmering glow behind a potted tree in the living room.

Henry charged toward the light, grabbed his magic book, and ducked behind the tree.

Pop! The medallion released from the cover and came to rest around his neck.

Then the book opened, and pages fluttered until they stopped on a spell for finding things.

The Come Back Here Spell

Has something important gone missing? Like your soccer cleats? Your homework? Or perhaps your pet has disappeared? Panic no more! This spell will bring back anything that's lost!

Ingredients:

1 flashlight
Something that
    looks like
    your missing item
1 drop of glue

Switch on the flashlight and pile the ingredients on top of each other. Hold your medallion in one hand and place the other hand over the mix. Chant the following spell.

> The magic search
> goes round and round!
> All lost items can be found!
> Bring my missing _____ to me!
> On the count of one, two, three!

Note: Stay focused on the Magic Cloud as well as the missing object, or the spell could grow out of control.

Henry tiptoed into his mom's office. He found a flashlight, glue, and a frog sticker.

Then he took everything
back behind the potted tree.
He switched on the flashlight
and placed
it on the
frog sticker.
Then he
squeezed a
drop of glue
on top and
chanted
the spell.

Poof! A cloud of magic appeared and swooshed away in search of the frog. It left a trail of sparkles in the air.

"Whoa," Henry said. "I love magic!"

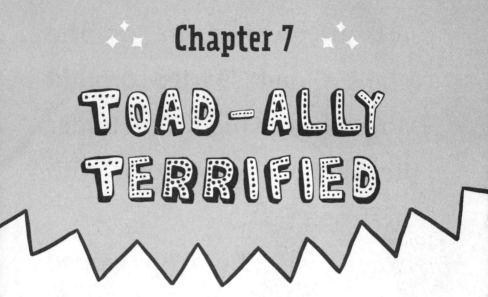

Chapter 7

TOAD-ALLY TERRIFIED

The Magic Cloud flew toward the kitchen.

Focus on the Magic Cloud and the frog, Henry reminded himself. *Focus on the Magic Cloud and the frog.*

Henry peeked in as the Magic Cloud swirled around Mom's legs, which were under the kitchen table along with the frog.

Ka-boing! The frog leaped into the Magic Cloud like a baseball bouncing into a glove.

Henry muffled a laugh—even though he was still *toad*-ally terrified! He had to stay focused on the cloud. He watched it float toward the ceiling above Mom and Ms. Mizzle!

Luckily, they were talking and didn't notice.

Come back to me! Henry thought, keeping his eyes on the Magic Cloud.

And the cloud listened! It flew toward Henry. The spell was going perfectly . . . until Dad opened the back door.

WHAM! The door smacked the Magic Cloud *and* the frog, batting them into the living room.

"I'm HOME!" Dad said.

Henry flattened himself against the wall and waited for a reaction from the kitchen. But the conversation continued normally.

Henry peeked into the kitchen—just to make sure. Yup. All was well.

WOW, that was WAY too close, Henry thought.

Then he turned around and looked in the living room . . . and knew his little frog problem had grown out of control.

Merg!

Merg!

Chapter 8

A RIBBIT-ING TALE

The good news was that there was no longer one frog in the living room. The bad news was that there were now hundreds of frogs. And they were doing what frogs do best. *Hopping.*

They hopped on the sofa. They hopped on the coffee table. They hopped on the windowsills, on the bookshelves, and in the fireplace. Henry put both hands on top of his head and looked around the room. What was he going to do?

Then the Magic Cloud swooped back to Henry.

"Can you please bring back the ONE Frog King?" he asked.

The Magic Cloud nodded, then swooshed through the room. It gathered all the frogs and turned them back into one perfectly plump frog.

Then the cloud laid the frog
onto Henry's waiting hands
and disappeared in a shower
of sparkles.

POOF!

"Ahem," said a voice from behind Henry. It was Mom, standing with her arms folded and one eyebrow raised. "This better not be what I *think* it is."

Uh-oh, thought Henry. But before he could explain, the frog leaped from his hands—*again.*

Sproing!

"Dudley! Max!"
Henry yelled. "We're
gonna need your
help!"
Henry's friends
zoomed down
the stairs,
blocking the frog's
escape, but
now it
hopped back
to the kitchen.

"Catch it!" Mom cried.

Henry closed in on the frog as it leaped toward Ms. Mizzle. But Ms. Mizzle was fast! She grabbed a dish towel and gently scooped up the frog. "Gotcha!" she said.

Max held Henry's bucket in front of Ms. Mizzle. The teacher gently placed the frog on the bottom. Then Henry covered

the bucket with plastic wrap and poked breathing holes with a fork.

"Well, Henry Heckelbeck," said Mom. "I'm sure you have a *ribbit*-ing tale to share with all of us."

Chapter 9
SMART FROG

Henry shared his frog tale, except for the part about casting a magical spell.

He told everyone how he'd spied the Frog King, caught him, and let him go.

He explained how the frog had somehow followed him home and up to his bedroom.

Then Henry braced himself for the worst punishment of his life.

But nobody shook a head or waved a finger.

Instead, his dad thoughtfully stroked his chin with his hand.

"That is one *smart* frog!" he finally said.

Everybody in the room nodded in agreement.

"How did it even get in the car?" Dudley asked.

"Or up the stairs?" added Max.

Mom walked over to Henry and wrapped her arms around him.

"I wish you'd felt you could've told me about your wonderful frog," she said. "Remember, I'm always here to help, especially when things hop out of control."

Henry shrugged. "I thought you'd get mad if you saw a frog in the house. Plus, I really thought I could handle it on my own."

Mom patted Henry on the shoulder. "Believe it or not, frogs don't freak me out," she said.

Everyone laughed.

"So, what do we do now?" asked Henry. "This frog clearly doesn't want to live in the creek . . . or in this bucket!"

Ms. Mizzle clasped her hands together. "You know," she began, "we really should have a class pet."

Henry, Dudley, and Max squealed at the same time.

"I LOVE that idea!" said Henry. "May I bring the frog to school tomorrow?"

"Absolutely!" said Ms. Mizzle. "Just make sure you don't lose it between now and then."

"Looks like we're going to have a new classmate!" said Max. "Nice going, Henry!"

Henry grinned from ear to ear. Max may have caught three frogs at the creek, but Henry had caught the new class pet.

Wow.

Chapter 10

THE FROG BOG

Mom drove Henry to school early to deliver the frog. Everybody gathered around the new glass tank in the classroom. It had a little pond, dirt, plants, and rocks.

Sitting on top of the biggest
rock was the Frog King.

"He even has his very own
swimming pool!" said Dudley.

"Also known as a frog bog!"
said Henry.

The class all buzzed with pure excitement. Ms. Mizzle introduced the class pet and told the adventure of how the frog had followed Henry home and tried to make a great frog escape by hopping all around the house.

"And now for the best part," Ms. Mizzle said, and paused. Henry gulped. Had she seen the magical moment of a million frogs?! Was she going to tell Henry's secret to the entire class?

Instead Ms. Mizzle said, "It's time to vote on a name for our new class pet."

The class rushed to their
seats, and Ms. Mizzle passed
out scrap paper.

The kids whispered and
giggled as they thought of
names for the class frog.

Henry quietly wrote down a few names: *The Frog King*, *Kermit*, *Pickles*, and *Dumpling*.

Ms. Mizzle let Henry collect the names in a basket.

"I'll write the names on the board," Ms. Mizzle said, "and then we'll vote for the one we like best."

She unfolded the slips of paper and began to laugh.

"We won't need to vote after all!" she said. "You've each agreed on a name already!"

Henry looked around the room. *But I didn't agree on a name!* he thought. *What is she talking about?*

"On the count of three, let's say the name together," said Ms. Mizzle. "One . . . two . . . three!"

"HENRY THE SECOND!" the class shouted as they gathered around Henry to clap and cheer.

"Chugga-wump-wump!" croaked the frog in agreement.

And that made Henry the happiest, *hoppy*-est kid in the whole school.

Check out the next book starring

HENRY HECKELBECK

HENRY HECKELBECK and the High-Dive Dare

"I'm ROASTING!" said Henry Heckelbeck.

"I'm BROILING!" said Dudley Day.

"Well, I'm BROASTING!" said Max Maplethorpe.

An excerpt from *Henry Heckelbeck and the High-Dive Dare*

"What's that?" asked Henry.

"It's a mix of roasting AND broiling," said Max. "Because today is the HOTTEST day in Brewster's history! My aunt said so, and she's a weather reporter on TV!"

Max picked up a pine cone from the floor of Dudley's tree house and pretended it was a microphone.

"Let's stay INSIDE today,

An excerpt from *Henry Heckelbeck and the High-Dive Dare*

Brewster!" she warned. "The weather is UGGY-MUGGY! With a one-hundred-percent chance of hot, sizzly, sweaty GROSSNESS."

The boys laughed.

"Maybe this will help," Dudley said. Then he reached for a bottle of lemonade he had brought from the kitchen. "Who wants some?"

An excerpt from *Henry Heckelbeck and the High-Dive Dare*